Ivy And Catalina Visit Cellville

Written by Cydnee Corujo & Shaneen Dials-Corujo

Illustrator: Atiyya NaDirah

This book is dedicated to the loving memory of my grandparents PaPa Victor Corujo, Grandma Lynette Davis, and Grandpa Morgan Davis. May our beautiful memories live on forever.

--Cydnee Corujo

This is Shanice, Ivy, and Catalina. Catalina and Ivy are super excited about visiting their grandparents. However their older sister, Shanice has plans so she will not be joining them. She wants her sisters to enjoy their time with their grandparents as she has in the past during her visits. Their grandparents live in a small town known as Cellville. It's Ivy and Catalina's first time visiting, so their grandparents are going to take them on a tour.

Mom and Dad finish packing the car and checking the house. As they leave Catalina asks, "Are we going to see Grandma Nette and Grandpa Morgan. "Yes we are," Mom responds. "We'll also visit PaPa Victor since he lives there too," Dad added.

Once they arrived, the family spent an entire day talking and eating at Grandma and Grandpa's. They listened to their grandparents talk about how Cellville was created and the purpose for its name. "As proud citizens of Cellville we are referred to as organelles," explained Grandpa.

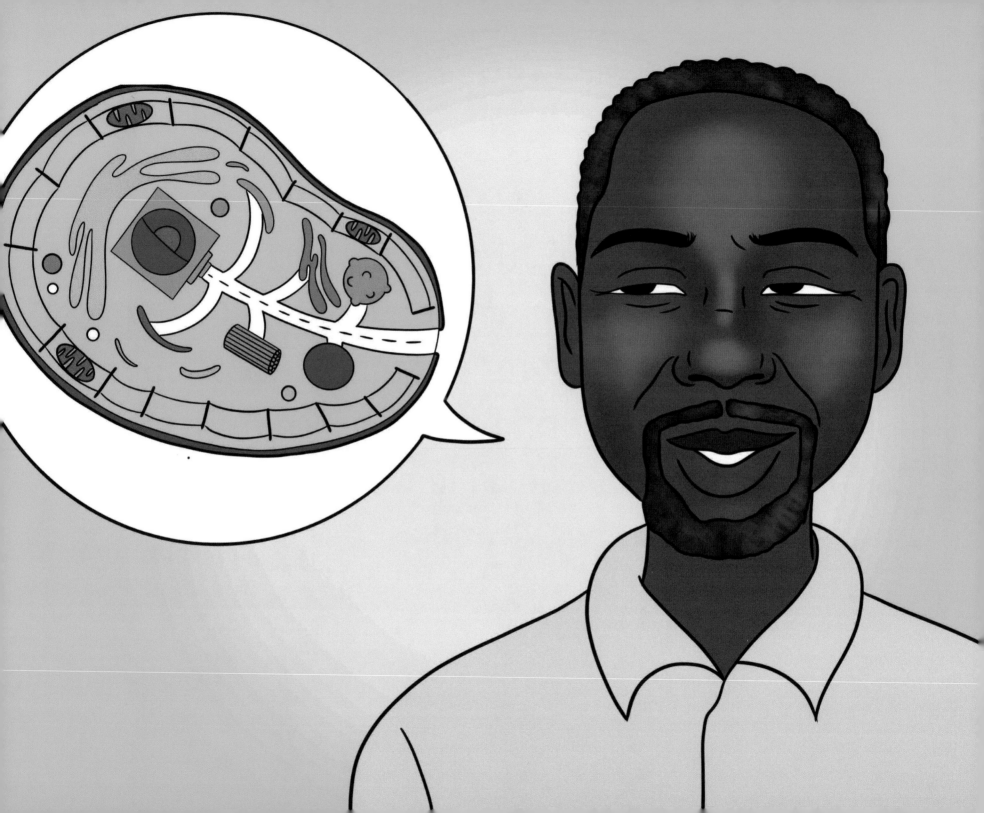

"As organelles, we live in the city and function in different capacities to help the city grow and thrive. Without organelles or citizens, Cellville would not exist," said Grandma. Grandpa explained, "The people of Cellville love science, so be sure to pay close attention during the tour tomorrow because everything has a function and meaning." Mom entered the room and said "Come along girls, you need to wash up and head to bed. Tomorrow is a big day for you all."

It was the next morning and the sun was shining brightly through the window. Catalina sat up with excitement. She tapped Ivy to wake her. Once Ivy was awake, the two girls got ready, and excitedly rushed downstairs to begin their adventure.

Ivy and Catalina headed out with their grandparents to see Cellville. "Let's start at the beginning of the city," Grandpa stated. This means we have to start near the welcome sign also known as the cell membrane. The cell membrane serves as the city border. It provides an entry and exit to the city just as the cell membrane controls what comes in and out of the cell.

If you look over the edge of the bridge you should see steel grinders and pipelines. Those grinders provide the structure of the city and the pipelines are the plumbing system. These structures are compared to the cytoskeleton of the cell. The cytoskeleton provides support, shape, and resistance for the contents of the cell.

Now, we'll stop at the Mayor's office which is like the nucleus of a cell. Just as the Mayor's office controls and decides what happens in a city, the nucleus controls the overall functions of the cell. Next door we have the Centriole Police Department. We rely on them as the protectors of our city, just as the cell relies on centrioles as its protection.

"I don't know about you girls, but we are hungry," Grandma stated. "Hey let's make a stop at the best food place in town, the Ribosome Restaurant," added Grandpa. "They are known for the different protein options that they provide as food for everyone, like the Ribosome does for the cell." "Hey Marty," yelled Grandpa. Marty waved as he rode pass on the back of the large truck. "Marty is my friend. He works for the Lysosome Garbage Company as a sanitation worker. He and his coworkers are responsible for clearing the waste from Cellville," Grandpa stated. The family ordered their food and sat down to eat.

Once the family finished eating, they headed home. As soon as they were in the yard, they noticed PaPa Victor's car. The girls jumped out of the car with excitement as they ran to greet him with hugs. PaPa smiled and hugged them back. "Hi, I hear you've been having a great time with Grandma and Grandpa," he stated. "We have PaPa, they showed us so many wonderful things," said Ivy. "That's great, now I get to show you the rest of Cellville," PaPa said.

As they drove, PaPa pointed out the many powerlines located on the street. "Regardless of where you are heading, in Cellville you must travel down Mitochondria Street also known as Main Street," said PaPa. "This is the area where the majority of the city's powerlines have been placed as it is the major energy or power source for Cellville. Just as the mitochondria is the powerhouse of the cell."

"You girls know that the highways that we are using to travel are important, right," asked PaPa. "Yes, because they allow us to move around the town from place-to-place," said Ivy. "That is correct" he said. "The highways of Cellville are like the Endoplasmic Reticulum. The ER is a passageway for proteins to move freely throughout the cell," explained PaPa.

"Hey girls, have you been paying attention to the beautiful lawns and other grassy areas throughout the city?" asked PaPa. "Yes sir," Catalina replied. "It fills the entire city and helps to make it beautiful, that's why we work hard to maintain it," he told them. The lawns in Cellville are like cyptoplasm because they act like the fluid that fills a cell.

"Let's make a quick stop at the Cellville Post Office. I am expecting a few packages," explained PaPa. As they entered the post office, they hear someone start speaking to PaPa. "Hi there, Victor how are you doing today?" the lady stated. "Hi Golgi, I'm well and how are you," PaPa replied. "I'm also well, and who are these little darlings?" Golgi asked. "These are two of my granddaughters, Ivy and Catalina," he responded.

"Girls, meet Ms. Golgi, she's the manager of the Post Office and one of my good friends," PaPa said. "What does the manager do?" Ivy asked. "As the manager, I make sure that everything is properly packaged before it leaves the post office," she responded. PaPa picked up his packages, thanked Golgi for her time, and said goodbye. As they were leaving he explained that the post office functions like the golgi apparatus of the cell since its main function in cells is to package molecules like fats and proteins.

"Well girls it seems that we have come to the last major stop in Cellville, it's time to head back to grandma and grandpa's," said PaPa. "I hope that you have had tons of fun and learned lots of new information." "We did PaPa," said Ivy. "Uh-huh," added Catalina.

The three arrived at grandma and grandpa's house. Mom and Dad met them with excitement. "Hi girls, I heard that you had lots of fun," said Mom. "We sure did," said Ivy. "This has been the best trip ever," said Catalina. "That's great girls, you don't know how happy your Mom and I are to hear that," Dad stated. "I cannot wait to tell all of my friends about our visit to the great town of Cellville," Ivy said excitedly. The family rested in preparation for their travel the next day.

The next day the family gave hugs and kisses to the grandparents and thanked them for showing them a great time. "Awww, we hate to see you all leave," said Grandma. "Its okay, we'll definitely come back to visit," Mom stated. "In the meantime, we have plenty of pictures to remind us of the Corujo Family's visit to Cellville."

The End

CPSIA information can be obtained at www.ICGtesting.com
Printed in the USA
BVIW120710230720
584112BV00027B/43